JEREM
WORRI
ABOUT
WIN

First published 2020 by Nosy Crow Ltd
The Crow's Nest, 14 Baden Place, Crosby Row, London SE1 1YW
www.nosycrow.com

ISBN 978 1 78800 774 0 (HB)
ISBN 978 1 78800 775 7 (PB)

Nosy Crow and associated logos are trademarks and/or
registered trademarks of Nosy Crow Ltd.

A CIP catalogue record for this book is available from the British Library.

Printed in China
Papers used by Nosy Crow are made from wood grown in sustainable forests.

10 9 8 7 6 5 4 3 2 1 (HB)
10 9 8 7 6 5 4 3 2 1 (PB)

For Albie, who loves the wind.
Love Mummy x
P.B.

For Huey
K.H.

JEREMY WORRIED ABOUT THE WIND

Pamela Butchart & Kate Hindley

nosy crow

Jeremy was a worrier.
He worried about everything.

He worried about . . .
odd socks,

shoe-eating worms,

too-crunchy crackers,

runaway dinosaurs,

burnt toast

and evil squirrels
(Jeremy was VERY
worried about squirrels).

He also worried about what would happen
if the zipper on his Big Coat got stuck.
It happened once.

So Jeremy never risked using the zipper
and was always EXTRA CAREFUL.

Jeremy worried about what would happen
if he ate a spotty banana.

So he stopped eating bananas
(even though bananas were his favourite).

Jeremy worried about what would happen if his shoelaces came undone. THAT could lead to SERIOUS DANGER.

So Jeremy took the laces out of all of his shoes.

But Jeremy's biggest worry wasn't spotty bananas OR runaway dinosaurs OR EVEN evil squirrels!

It was . . .

.... the WIND.

Jeremy was VERY worried about the wind.

One day, Jeremy met Maggie.

Jeremy noticed RIGHT AWAY that Maggie's
shoelaces were undone.

That's when he knew it was going to be up to him
to keep Maggie out of SERIOUS DANGER.
Otherwise, who KNOWS what would happen to her?

But Maggie wasn't scared of ANYTHING.
"What's the worst that could happen?" she said.

So Jeremy showed Maggie his list.

Soon, Jeremy and Maggie became best friends.
(Well, somebody had to look after her!)
Maggie was always trying to do SERIOUSLY
DANGEROUS THINGS like skipping or feeding pigeons.

But Jeremy was always there to show Maggie how to
be EXTRA CAREFUL and stay out of SERIOUS DANGER.

He taught her how to walk without falling through the cracks.

And how to eat crackers safely.

And how to avoid creepy, shoe-eating worms.

But Maggie didn't really listen.
"What's the worst that could happen?" she said.

One blustery day, Maggie wanted to play outside. So Jeremy did his WIDE EYES at Maggie and pointed to his Wind Dial.

"But I love the wind!" said Maggie. "It cleans the dust out of my ears and makes my hair grow long. Come on! What's the WORST that could happen?"

"Well," said Jeremy, but before he could finish, Maggie ran outside.

He had to SAVE HER!

But as soon as Jeremy stepped outside,
the wind caught in his Big Coat.

"HELP!" cried Jeremy as a great big gust of wind blew him RIGHT out of his shoes and up into the sky.

The moment Jeremy arrived home,
he saw Maggie.

"Maggie!"
he shouted . . .

"I landed on top of the HIGHEST mountain and WHIZZED through the snow with SLED DOGS, was SAVED by a NARWHAL, then got captured by PIRATES and flew home in a MAGICAL FLYING MACHINE!

And . . .

. . . it was BRILLIANT!

And I want to do it AGAIN!" cried Jeremy.
"Come on . . ."

"But what about the SERIOUS DANGER?"
said Maggie.

"Well," said Jeremy, "what's the **WORST** that could happen?"

First published in the UK in 2012

This edition first published in 2022 by
Pavilion Children's Books
43 Great Ormond Street
London WC1N 3HZ
An imprint of Pavilion Books Company Limited

Design and layout © 2012, 2022 Pavilion Children's Books
Text and illustrations © 2012, 2022 Frann Preston-Gannon

ISBN: 978-1-84365-516-9

A CIP catalogue record for this book is available from the British Library.

10 9 8 7 6 5 4 3 2 1

Reproduction by Mission, Hong Kong
Printed and bound by Toppan Leefung Ltd, China

For my Mother
and Father

The Journey home

Frann Preston-Gannon

PAVILION

Dear Reader,

When I first had the idea for *The Journey Home* back in 2011 I had never written a book before. I studied illustration for three years at university and had grand dreams of becoming a children's author, but I hadn't found the right subject until then.

I was absent-mindedly sketching different things in a notebook when I noticed a small polar bear in a boat looking up at me from the pages. I started to think about him and what his story might be.

That small bear held out his paw and took me on a journey that would eventually become the story you hold in your hands. From first meeting the bear I knew that the story might not be the happiest, but I hoped it would be a tale that got children thinking, that started conversations and encouraged kindness towards the creatures we share this planet with.

This edition marks ten years since *The Journey Home* was first published and the issues in this story are more important than ever. The human impact on the climate and the wildlife of this planet is undeniable.

This is one of the first storyboards I drew for *The Journey Home*

We know the need to protect these animals and their habitats is crucial not just for the survival of these species, but also for humans. We share one planet. When it comes to our future, just like the four animals in this book, we are all in the same boat.

Very best,

Frann x

The frozen sea was melting. 'Where has all of my ice gone?' the Polar Bear wondered. 'And where is my food?' He looked around. 'Well, I can't stay here,' he decided, so he went for a swim.

As he swam along he found a little boat, alone upon the sea.

'This will be easier than swimming,' he thought as he climbed in.

Before long he came upon a city where machines rumbled and tall buildings hid the sky.

'What are you doing?' asked a Panda watching from the docks.

'I am sailing in my boat,' replied the Polar Bear. 'It's easier than swimming, you see.'

'Well, I can't stay here,' said the Panda lowering himself down into the boat. 'I think I'll come with you.'

And together the two animals sailed along,
listening to the seagulls and saying hello to the fish.

After a while, they floated up a river to where a jungle used to be. 'I've nothing to climb anymore,' said an Orangutan. 'My trees are disappearing.'

The Panda and the Polar Bear looked around and saw that she was right.

'Well, you could join us if you like?' said the Panda. 'Perhaps we will spot some trees along the way.' So she climbed in and off they went.

As they sailed on, they looked up at the sky and saw the beautiful shapes the clouds had made.

'What's that behind the rock?' said the Orangutan suddenly.

'Shsshhh...' said an Elephant. 'I'm trying to hide. Someone's trying to steal my tusks.'

'Why don't you come with us?' whispered the Panda. 'We can sail far away from here.'

So the Elephant climbed in too.

And so the animals laughed and played as their small boat carried them further and further. But the sea started to swell and dark clouds appeared in the sky.

The storm
passed and the animals
knew the terrible waves had carried
them far far away. They thought of their
homes and how much they missed
them. As they sailed on they
all felt very lost on the
big blue sea.

A Dodo watched from his
island as the boat and its animals
came into view. 'Hello there!'
he called to them as they
sailed closer.

'We're lost!' shouted the
Polar Bear to the Dodo.
'We've sailed too far and now
we want to go home.'

'Well of course you can
go home!' said the Dodo.

'Really?' said the animals together.
'When?'

'You can go home when
the trees grow back
and when the ice returns
and when the cities stop
getting bigger and
when the hunting stops.'

'Oh,' said the Orangutan
thoughtfully.

'And when will that be?' asked the Polar Bear.

'I don't know,' said the Dodo.
'Let's see what tomorrow brings.'

Now you have read the story,
think about some of the
questions below

1. Where do the Polar Bear, Panda, Orangutan
and Elephant each live? What do their homes
have to include for the animals to live happily?

2. What things do we need in our own homes to be happy?

3. Why might the Polar Bear's ice be melting?

4. Why do you think the Panda doesn't feel at home
in the city?

5. Why do humans cut down trees? How can this
be done with less damage to the environment?

6. What do you think might make the Elephant feel more safe in its home?

7. What do you hope the future will bring for the animals?

Follow that boat!

What route do you think the animals would have taken in their boat around the world? Start in the icy Arctic and with your finger trace the route that you think they would have taken.

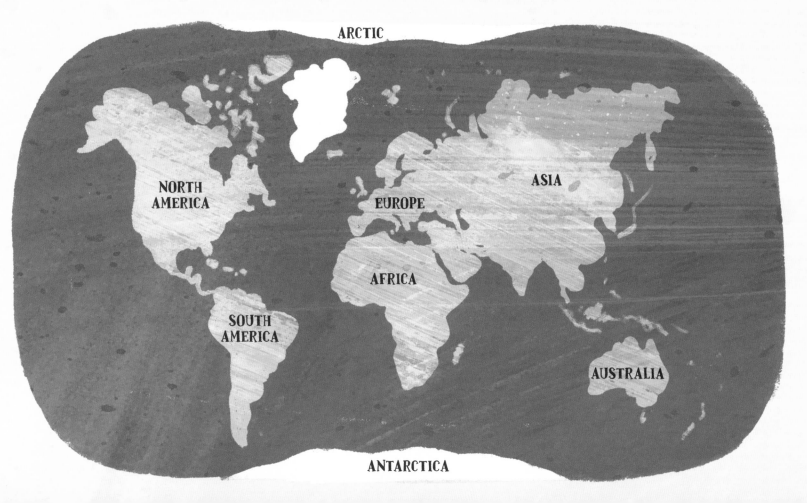

Animal facts

Polar Bear
Habitat: Arctic
Food: Fish, seals
Status: Vulnerable
Threats: Climate change is causing the Earth to heat up. This is causing the ice to melt in the Arctic leaving polar bears with less chance to hunt for food.

Panda
Habitat: Mountains of Central China
Food: Bamboo
Status: Vulnerable
Threats: The panda's natural habitat is often destroyed for farming and tourism. They are also under threat from poaching.

Orangutan
Habitat: Rainforests of Borneo and Sumatra.
Food: Fruit and leaves, sometimes insects and birds' eggs
Status: Critically endangered
Threats: Deforestation of its home, often for palm oil which is used in many products humans use

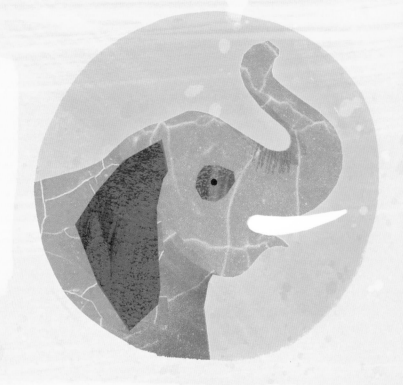

Elephant
Habitat: African savannah or forests. Jungles of Asia.
Food: Roots, grasses, fruit and bark
Status: All types of African and Asian elephants are endangered or critically endangered
Threats: Hunting for ivory (tusks), loss of habitat

Dodo
Habitat: Mauritius
Food: Fruit, nuts and seeds
Status: Extinct
Threats: Dodos were entirely wiped out when Europeans arrived on their island. Their forest home was cut down and they were hunted for food.

Good news

It might feel like these animals, rightly, don't have a very good impression of humans and how they treat the planet. However, there are lots of people working very hard to try to protect animals and their environments. Here is some good news from recent years.

Panda

Thanks to huge efforts by conservationists to protect their habitat, scientists say that the number of pandas has been increasing over the last thirty years. This has meant that in 2016 the panda was moved from 'endangered' to 'vulnerable' on the global list of species at risk of extinction. The increase in the panda population shows that when people come together and work hard we can help save endangered species, although there is still lots of work to do.

Elephant

While elephant numbers still face a big threat from poaching and loss of habitat there has been some fantastic news in recent years. In 2020 the Kenya Wildlife Service said that the number of elephants in that country had more than doubled in thirty years, increasing from 16,000 in 1989 to 34,800 by the end of 2019, and in 2020 a whopping 140 elephants were born in Amboseli National Park. The rise is partly thanks to the country's efforts to stop the poaching of elephants. In northern Kenya, elephant poaching in protected areas has reduced by 35% since 2012. When governments and communities come together they can help endangered species to recover.

Polar Bear

Since this book was first published, leaders from the countries where polar bears live have agreed to work together to help the bears. In the past ten years, the number of polar bears has increased, and in Canada in particular the populations seem to be growing well. However, unless we work together to stop the melting of sea ice, the numbers of polar bears could once again start to decrease.

Orangutan

In Borneo, large areas of rainforest are now protected, and orangutan numbers have increased. Also, over the last ten years, many companies have promised to stop using palm oil from deforested areas, one of the greatest threats to orangutans. However, illegal logging and wildlife trading are still big problems — we need to keep working to protect these beautiful great apes, and their homes.

Project ideas

1. Film a news report on the plight of these endangered animals.

2. Pretend to be one of the animals and write a letter to humans explaining why they should help protect your home.

3. Make a poster encouraging people to take care of wildlife and hang it somewhere such as your window, local library or school (with permission).

4. Why not write and illustrate a sequel to The Journey Home? What do you hope happens next for these animals? Do they manage to get to their homes?

What can your family do to help look after the environment?

Cycle or walk rather than drive

Reduce food waste and eat less meat

Check the products you buy do not contain unsustainable palm oil

Avoid buying single-use plastic